The Ghost in the Computer

The Bobbsey Twins®

THE GHOST
IN THE
COMPUTER

Laura Lee Hope

Illustrated by John Speirs

WANDERER BOOKS
Published by
Simon & Schuster, Inc., New York

Copyright © 1984 by Simon & Schuster, Inc.
All rights reserved
including the right of reproduction
in whole or in part in any form
Published by WANDERER BOOKS
A Division of Simon & Schuster, Inc.
Simon & Schuster Building
1230 Avenue of the Americas
New York, New York 10020

Manufactured in the United States of America
10 9 8 7 6 5 4 3 2 1
10 9 8 7 6 5 4 3 2 pbk

THE BOBBSEY TWINS, WANDERER and colophon
are registered trademarks of Simon & Schuster, Inc.

Library of Congress Cataloging in Publication Data

Hope,Laura Lee.
    The ghost in the computer.

    (The Bobbsey twins; 10)
    Summary: The Bobbsey twins learn to use a computer
and apply their detective skills to a mystery involving
a clown, a ghost, and a prize won at a school fair.
    [1. Mystery and detective stories. 2. Computers—
Fiction] I. Title. II. Series: Hope, Laura Lee.
Bobbsey twins (1980-   ); 10.
PZ7.H772Gh 1984   [Fic]   83-23303
ISBN 0-671-43591-4 (pbk.)

Contents

1.	A Spooky Light	7
2.	Fun Day	15
3.	The Runaway Ghost	30
4.	Bimbo Vanishes!	43
5.	The Motel Clue	56
6.	Sidewalk Bully	69
7.	Startling News	80
8.	The Red-Nosed Clown	91
9.	Secret Hobby	99
10.	Computer Room Mystery	109
11.	Surprise Prize	117

·1·

A Spooky Light

"Gee, Bert, I didn't realize we'd stayed at the library so long!" Nan Bobbsey said.

"Neither did I," said Bert, "till I looked at the clock and saw how late it was."

"It must be going on nine by now," Nan fretted as they bicycled along in the deep gathering dusk. "We were supposed to be home twenty minutes ago!"

It was a lovely June evening. The pretty dark-haired girl and her twelve-year-old twin brother had been doing some end-of-term schoolwork at the Lakeport Public Library.

"Never mind," Bert said hopefully. "When we show Mom and Dad our finished reports, they'll . . ." Suddenly his voice took on a strange tone. "Nan, look!" he pointed.

"Yes, Bert, I know," Nan said, laughing in spite of herself. "There's our school."

"Don't be funny! Look at that center window. Don't you see the light in there?"

Nan gasped as she noticed the faint glimmer. "Oh, yes—and it's moving! Bert, someone's in the school who shouldn't be there! What should we do?"

"Bike on home fast and tell Mom or Dad. They can call the police. I'll stay and keep watch till the cops come."

"Okay." Without another word, Nan sped off homeward. On arriving, she leaned her bike against the front porch steps and dashed into the house. "Mom, Dad!" she exclaimed breathlessly. "Bert and I saw a light moving around inside the school. He's keeping watch until someone else gets there. He thought you might want to call the police!"

"Better sit down and catch your breath, dear." Mrs. Bobbsey patted the sofa seat next to where she was sitting. "Daddy will deal with it."

Mr. Bobbsey nodded and put down the evening paper as he rose from his easy chair and started toward the phone. "Yes, I think we had better call the police. There may be vandals in the building."

Freddie, Nan's six-year-old brother, jumped up from the floor, where he had been putting pieces of a puzzle away in their box. "If the police come, I want to go see what happens!"

"Now, Freddie, it's past your bedtime," said his mother. "You should have gone up to get ready for bed five minutes ago, when Flossie did." Flossie was his little twin sister.

"Aw, gee." He glumly resumed picking up the puzzle.

"And I think you'd better hurry, too,

young man," Mrs. Bobbsey advised, smiling at him.

"Well, the police are on their way. We'd better go get Bert," said Mr. Bobbsey, returning from the hallway after hanging up the phone. "Nan, maybe you'd better come along and help me spot Bert."

Blond, curly-haired Freddie jumped up again eagerly. "I'll help you find him, Daddy! Can I come too, please? . . . Oh, please!"

"Sorry, young fella, it's bedtime for you." Mr. Bobbsey chuckled and patted the little boy's shoulder. "But if you're good, I'll come up and tell you all about it when we get back."

A few minutes later, Mr. Bobbsey stopped the car in the school driveway. Bert came hurrying up to join him and Nan. "The light was moving up the front stairs when Nan and I first saw it, but now it's on the second floor," he reported. "See up there?"

Sure enough, a glow could be seen behind the closed, slatted blinds!

"That's the computer room, where the teaching machines are," Nan said in a low voice.

Just then a police car arrived and slid to a stop close by. As two officers jumped out and slammed the car doors, the light in the school went out!

The policemen quickly unlocked the front door of the building, and they all went inside. Bert and Nan led the way upstairs to the computer room. But when one officer switched on the room lights, it was empty!

He and his partner made a swift search of all the second-floor classrooms without finding any sign of the intruder.

"Looks like our night bird has flown," he said.

"Let's check the first floor, anyway," the other officer replied.

The group started down the front stairway. Just as they reached the foot of the stairs, they heard the office telephone ring. One policeman went to answer it.

Emerging from the office a moment later, he said, "It's your wife, Mr. Bobbsey." Then he and his partner went off to complete their search.

Nan and Bert accompanied their father into the office and waited as he picked up the phone. He listened for a minute and then said, "Well, don't worry, dear. We'll find him."

He hung up and turned to the older twins. "Your mother says Freddie's disappeared. She thinks he sneaked out and headed this way, so as not to miss out on any excitement."

"That Freddie!" Bert said.

Nan forced a smile, hoping to ease her father's anxiety. "He's some little brother!"

By now the police officers were coming back through the hall, after completing their hasty search of the first-floor classrooms with no result. So they and the Bobbseys left the school together.

On the front walk outside stood a white-faced little boy, his eyes wide as saucers.

"Freddie!" Nan cried, running up to him anxiously. "What's the matter?"

"I just saw a ghost!" he blurted.

·2·

Fun Day

"A ghost!" said one of the policemen with a smile. "Sure you aren't imagining things, sonny?"

"N-n-no, sir. I really saw it!" Freddie's lower lip trembled, but his tone of voice convinced everyone that he had really seen something scary.

"What did this ghost look like, Freddie?" his father asked.

"S-sort of whitish! I couldn't see very well in the dark, but it scooted off that way!" The little boy pointed toward some bushes.

"Nan, you take Freddie back to the car, please," Mr. Bobbsey said. "The rest of us will search for whatever or whomever it was that scared him."

Nan did as her father directed, while he and Bert and the officers hurried toward the bushes and shrubbery that screened one side of the school grounds. Here they spread out to hunt the spook.

The policemen each had flashlights, and Mr. Bobbsey had also brought one from the car. Bert was the only searcher with no beam to shine ahead.

Suddenly, as he passed a tree, something got in his way. Bert tripped and almost went sprawling, but he grabbed the tree trunk just in time.

A mocking laugh reached his ears. It faded off into the gloom before he could straighten up again. Bert ran toward the sound.

Far ahead, he glimpsed a dim fleeing figure and heard faint hoots of laughter.

Both were soon swallowed up in the dark. Bert finally gave up the hopeless chase and went back to the school.

"I think it was just some kid playing a trick," he reported, and showed his dad and the policemen the stick that had been used to trip him.

"That figures." One officer nodded. "We'll keep an eye on the school to make sure no vandals come back."

Bert had a strong hunch that the prankster was Danny Rugg, a bully in his own grade. But he felt it was not fair to accuse Danny without proof.

Flossie was wide-awake and waiting up with her mother when the other three Bobbseys returned home.

"What happened?" she asked excitedly.

"I saw a ghost!" Freddie exclaimed.

Flossie's blue eyes opened wide. "Did he *really*, Daddy?"

"Well . . . someone came running out of

the school, and whatever he had on looked white to Freddie—but Bert and I think it was just some youngster playing a trick." Mr. Bobbsey picked up his little girl and bounced her high in the air as Flossie squealed and giggled. "So my little fat fairy needn't start worrying about any spooks popping out at her when she goes back to school Monday!"

Dinah Johnson, the black lady who helped Mrs. Bobbsey cook and keep house, made cocoa for everyone. Then Mrs. Bobbsey said, "Now up to bed, all you twins! Remember, tomorrow will be one Saturday morning when you don't want to sleep late—because you all know what day it will be!"

"Fun Day, Fun Day!" cried Freddie, hopping and skipping as he led the bedtime parade upstairs.

Saturday morning dawned sunny and bright, just right for the School Fair. This was put on each year by the Parent-

Teachers Association to raise money for extra school activities. It was always held on the last Saturday before summer vacation—or "Fun Day," as everyone called it.

The Bobbseys were all in high spirits. Soon after breakfast they set out for the fair, meeting other families on the way.

Mrs. Bobbsey and Dinah had each made a cake for the bake sale, which was to be held in the gym. But most of the fun was going on outdoors.

Booths and counters of all kinds had been set up on the school grounds. A minisized merry-go-round and Ferris wheel had been hired for the day, run by men in blue-and-white-striped jackets. They had also brought a Shetland pony, which could be ridden around the playground.

Balloons and banners fluttered all about the school. Within minutes, it seemed, after the fair opened, the whole scene was ablaze with color and noisy with laughter and happy voices.

Bimbo the Clown was on hand to perform, as he did every year. His face was made up with a big red nose, white circles around his eyes, and a wild yellow wig. His costume consisted of a squashed top hat, an out-at-the-elbow coat, and oversized shoes that were coming apart at the toes. A circle of children surrounded him, howling with merriment as he capered about, doing funny tricks.

"Oh, I just *love* Bimbo!" cried Flossie, clapping her hands. He used his cane to scratch his back and tip his hat to a lady, then almost toppled over when he tried to lean on it.

"Who is Bimbo really, Daddy?" asked Freddie. "I mean, where does he live and what does he do all the rest of the time, when he's not being a clown on Fun Day?"

"Good question," said Mr. Bobbsey,

grinning and clapping with the rest of the audience. "All anyone knows is that he shows up every year and performs free, to help make the fair a success. I guess he just enjoys making people laugh."

There was a loud *honk*! as Bimbo tweaked the big red bulge at the tip of his nose. This sent his fans into fresh gales of laughter.

Just then, the school principal spoke into a microphone, his voice blaring from loudspeakers on the school lawn. "Your attention, please, everyone! May I introduce—*Mister Checkers*!"

"Mister Checkers" turned out to be one of the classroom computers, with a funny face mounted on top. A checkerboard lay on the table in front of the computer, and a plump boy, about ten years old, was standing beside it.

"Hey, that's Rodney Blake," Bert murmured.

"I know," Nan replied. "He's really a whiz with computers!"

"He doesn't look very happy with all these people staring at him."

"I guess he's shy," said Nan. She looked sympathetic. "Rodney's awfully smart, but he never seems to have any friends."

"Or much fun, either, poor guy," Bert added.

It turned out that Rodney had programmed the computer to play checkers! For twenty-five cents a game, anyone could try to beat Mister Checkers and win a prize. A checkerboard pattern on the screen showed every move.

Two people played and lost. The parents who were watching were amazed that a ten-year-old schoolboy could program a computer so expertly.

"Is this the computer that scientist promised to give to the school?" Mrs. Bobbsey whispered.

Bert shook his head. "No, this is one of the regular computers we get lessons and tests on."

The scientist—Professor Tate of Midwest University—had promised to donate a larger and more powerful computer from his own laboratory to the school. It had already been delivered.

"But that one won't be officially presented to the school till graduation day next Wednesday," Nan told her mother.

The next person to try his luck at the checkers game was Danny Rugg. But it soon became clear that he stood little chance of winning. On his third move, Mister Checkers jumped and captured two of his pieces. Soon Danny had lost almost half his men, where as Mister Checkers had lost only one and already had three kings crowned.

By this time many onlookers had lost interest and moved on. The principal had also walked away to act as "barker" for another fair attraction.

Seeing this, Danny Rugg jumped up with a sulky look and swept all the pieces off the board. "You're cheating!" he said to Rodney Blake.

"No, I'm not," said Rodney. "The computer decides what moves Mister Checkers should make."

"You programmed it to cheat!" Danny insisted and doubled up his fists as if to hit the fat boy.

Rodney's face turned pale. He looked afraid of the bully, who was bigger and stronger than he was. Bert Bobbsey stepped in between them.

"Let him alone, Danny!" Bert ordered sharply. "You're just mad because you're losing."

Danny scowled angrily. But he knew he was in the wrong, and he also knew that the Bobbsey boy could not be bullied. "If we ever fight, *you'll* be the one who loses!" he blustered.

"Try me and we'll see," Bert said calmly.

Instead, Danny muttered something

under his breath and stalked off with a jeering laugh. Bert felt surer than ever now that Danny was the sneak who had tripped him in the dark.

Meanwhile, Flossie had wandered off to a booth where a PTA lady painted funny faces on her kid customers. "Honey, you're so cute," she said to the little girl, "I think you'd make a wonderful kewpie doll!"

So she painted big eyelashes and round pink cheeks and red cupid's-bow lips on the little upturned face. Flossie giggled with delight when she saw herself in the mirror.

Just then Bimbo the Clown passed by. "Ah, my beautiful princess!" he cried. Seizing her by one hand, with his other arm behind her waist, he waltzed Fossie around and around while she gasped and squealed and laughed. Then he pulled a bag of red heart-shaped peppermint candies from his pocket and offered her one, exclaiming with a bow, "You have stolen my heart, dear lady!"

The onlookers applauded as Flossie happily popped the candy in her mouth, and Bimbo tweaked his big red nose with a loud *honk*!

By now all four twins had wandered off on their own. After checking out various booths, Freddie decided to try fishing for a prize in the "Fish Pond."

This was a large box with cardboard fish inside it. Each had a wire ring attached. Players could pick up any fish they could catch with a hook and line. If there was a number on the bottom of the fish, it meant the player won a prize.

Freddie hooked an orange sunfish. When he turned it over, he saw the number 17.

"Good for you, dear! You've won a prize!" said Mrs. Mason. She and her husband were tending the booth. They were the parents of Bert's friend, Charlie Mason.

"Well now, let's see what you've won, Freddie," said Mr. Mason. He scanned the row of prizes and came to a white envelope bearing a big red numeral 17 on it. "Aha, here we are!"

Freddie opened the envelope, but since he could not yet read very well, he asked for help. "Please tell me what this paper says, Mr. Mason."

"By George, you've won the mystery prize, Freddie!"

"What's that?" the little boy asked.

"Hmm, I don't know yet. The paper says to look for a red paper-wrapped package in the first-floor storeroom. Come on, we'll go and see!"

Hand in hand, Mr. Mason and Freddie hurried into the school through the front door, then to the left down the hall to the storeroom. But there was no red paper-wrapped package there!

"What's happened to it?" Freddie asked.

Before Mr. Mason could reply, they heard an angry scuffle outside—then a loud *thumpety-thump-thump-thump*!

· 3 ·

The Runaway Ghost

"What was that?" cried Freddie.

"Sounded like someone fell downstairs!" Mr. Mason's faced showed alarm. "I'd better go see."

He dashed out of the storeroom with Freddie following close behind. A lady was hurrying toward the stairwell from the other end of the hall. She was one of the mothers in charge of the bake sale. Freddie remembered seeing her when Mrs. Bobbsey and Dinah took their cakes to the gym.

"Who fell?" Mr. Mason called out to her.

"Bimbo the Clown," she replied anxiously. "Only he didn't fall—he was pushed! Oh, dear, I'm afraid he may be hurt!" As she reached the stairwell, she gasped and pointed down the steps.

Bimbo lay sprawled on the basement landing!

All three rushed to help him. Mr. Mason reached the clown first. Bimbo groaned slightly but did not move as Mr. Mason felt his pulse. "Let's hope he didn't hit his head too hard! Did you say he was *pushed,* Mrs. Cole?"

The lady nodded with a shocked expression. "Yes, I was just coming around the corner from the gym when I saw him struggling with a man!"

Mr. Mason stared in surprise. "You mean they were fighting or punching each other?"

"Well, not exactly. Bimbo had a box in his hand that was wrapped in red paper, and the other man was trying to grab it away. Finally he gave Bimbo a hard shove to make him let go. That's when poor Bimbo tumbled downstairs!"

A box wrapped in red paper! Freddie's eyes bugged wide at Mr. Mason, who nodded tensely. "Yes, that must have been your mystery prize, Freddie. Sounds like Bimbo was trying to save it from being stolen."

He turned back to Mrs. Cole and said quickly, "What did the thief look like?"

"I couldn't see his face very well, but he had on a blue-and-white-striped jacket. He ran off down that corridor across from the stairwell."

"I'll try to catch him. Freddie, you go and get Officer Tompkins!"

"Yes, sir!" As Mr. Mason started after the crook, Freddie ran outside to find the neighborhood policeman. Officer Tompkins was usually on hand at Fun Day every year, just to see that everything stayed orderly and also to help.

On hearing Freddie's story, he hurried to investigate. But neither he nor Mr. Mason could spot the thief or even find anyone who had caught a glimpse of the fleeing crook.

"Never mind, we may not have far to look," muttered Officer Tompkins. "That blue-and-white-striped jacket sounds like one of the ride attendants."

But this clue, too, proved a false hope. The men who operated the minirides were all on the job, and none had left their posts. It turned out, however, that an extra jacket had been stolen from their vans. The thief had used it as a disguise.

"No wonder he got away," said Mr. Mason. "All he had to do was take off that jacket. Without it, there was no other way to spot hm."

Officer Tompkins tilted his cap to scratch his head. "By golly, this is the first time any such thing's ever happened on Fun Day." He heaved a sigh of disgust. "Oh, well, let's see how Bimbo is."

By the time they walked back into the school, the clown was sitting upright, propped against the wall of the landing. The bake sale lady was holding a glass to his lips as he sipped some water.

"I'd better drive him to the hospital," said Officer Tompkins.

"Yes, indeed," Mr. Mason agreed. "It's a good idea to have a doctor check him over."

"Think you can stand up, Bimbo?" Freddie asked.

The clown still looked dazed, but managed to struggle to his feet. The policeman and Freddie helped him walk outside to Officer Tompkins's car in the teachers' parking lot.

"I'll be back soon, Freddie," the policeman promised. "Then we'll do some more detective work and try to find your prize."

Bimbo opened his eyes and winked at Freddie as the police car drove off.

Meanwhile, news of the robbery had

spread quickly. The other Bobbsey twins were already doing some detective work of their own. Freddie found Nan, Bert, and Flossie talking to two little kindergarten girls. The pair had been swinging on the playground swings until a few moments ago. Both were wide-eyed and chattering away excitedly.

"Know why we left?" one said to Freddie when she saw they had a new listener. "A funny-looking ghost came out of the back door of the school and ran off through the trees!"

"We didn't want to stay out in back any longer after that," said the other. "It was too scary!"

The girls said the ghost was all white—even its hands and face! Nan started around the corner of the school playground. "Come on, twins. Let's go back there and check."

On the cement stoop, just outside the back door, they found traces of whitish powder.

"Hmm, looks like that phony ghost left a trail," said Bert. He opened the door. Sure enough, there was more white stuff on the floor inside.

Nan rubbed some between her fingers. "I'll bet that's *flour!*" she exclaimed. "If I'm right, it may have come from the home ec room!"

Her guess proved a good one. The trail led to the home economics room where the girls did cooking. Inside, the flour bin was open and a good deal of flour spilled about. Also, still hanging on a hook nearby was one of the teacher's white smocks.

"Smart guy," said Bert. "Just came in here and grabbed a coat to wear, and then smeared himself with flour. . . . Some ghost!"

Nan agreed. "It was certainly a good way to keep anyone from recognizing him."

Officer Tompkins soon returned. When the twins showed him the flour trail, he said they had done some mighty fine detective work. "But if we're ever going to track down that mystery prize, our first problem is to find out what it was."

"How can we find out?" Freddie said forlornly. "I never even got a chance to open it."

"Never mind," said Flossie. "Maybe the people at the Fish Pond will know." Trying to cheer up her brother, the little blond girl put her arm around his shoulder and looked at him earnestly.

Flossie still had her kewpie-doll face painted on. She looked so funny that Freddie laughed and hugged her. Officer Tompkins chuckled, too. "Your sister's right, Freddie," he said. "Let's see what we can find out at the Fish Pond."

Mr. and Mrs. Mason were able to tell them very little. They explained that the mystery prize was donated every year by Miss Samantha Wagby.

"We never know what it is until the winner opens it," said Mrs. Mason. "But it's always a very nice prize, usually something quite expensive. Miss Wagby is quite rich, you see, and very kindhearted—especially to children."

"Well then, I guess our next step is to talk to Miss Wagby," said Officer Tompkins and he started toward his police car. "Come on, kids!"

Miss Wagby lived in a big old mansion with trees all around it. Several moments after Officer Tompkins rang the bell, a kindly faced middle-aged woman with an apron over her dress opened the door. The policeman asked to speak to Miss Wagby.

"I'm sorry," she said. "Miss Wagby is not here. She's in the hospital. I'm Mrs. Sykes, her housekeeper." Then she smiled at the twins and opened the door wider. "But come in, anyway. Maybe I can help you."

As they entered, the twins looked about the big, dark-paneled hall with interest. It was cool and quiet, and in the old-fashioned rooms on each side of the hallway they could see shelves and cabinets containing all sorts of little statues and china figures and carved ornaments.

Nan, who enjoyed her art class in school, gazed at the display admiringly. "Are some of those carvings jade?" she asked Mrs. Sykes.

"Yes, dear. Miss Wagby has been collecting the things you see for years. I don't know much about them myself, but I'm sure she'd love to show them to you someday when she's well."

After learning why Officer Tompkins and the twins had come, the housekeeper shook her head regretfully. "I'm afraid I can't help you, after all. You see, I wasn't here when the prize was sent over to the school. I was visiting my sister in Cleveland. In fact, I only got back on Thursday, after Miss Wagby was taken to the hospital."

"Then you've no idea what the prize was?"

"No, I'm sorry." Mrs. Sykes looked slightly puzzled as she added, "I do know what Mrs. Wagby was planning to give at first—but apparently she changed her mind. I imagine the maid who filled in while I was away actually wrapped the prize and took it over to the school."

Mrs. Sykes paused suddenly and knit her brows. "Wait a minute, now! Maybe Mr. Gresham would know. He's the handyman and gardener. Miss Wagby might have had *him* take the prize to the school."

She excused herself to go and fetch Mr. Gresham. He was an elderly man in a flannel work shirt and khaki trousers. It turned out he had, indeed, taken the mystery prize to the school. But he, too, had no idea what was in the red paper-wrapped box.

"You'd have to ask Miss Sanchez about

that," he told the visitors. "She worked here as the temporary maid while Mrs. Sykes was gone."

"Any idea how we can get in touch with her?" Bert spoke up.

"Well now, I know she came from the Gem Employment Agency, if that's any help."

While the housekeeper went off to look up the agency's address, Mr. Gresham noticed Freddie's glum expression. "You the one who would have gotten the prize? Never mind, sonny," he said in a kindly voice. "I have a surprise for you that'll help make up for your disappointment!"

· 4 ·

Bimbo Vanishes!

Freddie's face brightened. "What kind of a surprise?" he asked.

"Would you like to see it right now?"

"Yes, sir—I would!"

Mr. Gresham chuckled and put a hand on Freddie's shoulder. "Come along then, young fellow!"

"May I come, too?" begged Flossie.

"You certainly may, honey." The handyman led the two little twins outside and among the tall shade trees that surrounded Miss Wagby's mansion. One tree had a wooden ladder leading up into its leafy heights. The handyman stopped near it and, with a smile, pointed upward. "How'd you like to play up there, sonny?"

Nestled on a stout branch was a lovely tree house, with a fenced-in porch around it!

"Ooh, it's bee-yoo-tiful!" squealed Flossie.

The elderly handyman explained that the tree house had been built long ago for a nephew of Miss Wagby's, who often came to visit her. Freddie wanted to clamber up the ladder at once. But then he saw that two rungs were missing, and the wooden upright on one side had split apart.

"It's broken!" he lamented.

"Yep, but here's your surprise," said Mr. Gresham. "I'm going to fix that ladder right now, so you two can play up there this afternoon."

"Hooray!" shouted Freddie. "That's a *super* surpise!"

"Thank you ever so much!" said Flossie.

"Me, too! Thanks a lot, Mr. Gresham," her brother added, remembering his manners.

The kind-hearted handyman beamed as the little twins hopped about and clapped their hands.

When they got back to the house, Freddie and Flossie learned from the older twins that Officer Tompkins had just found out from the employment agency the telephone number and address of Miss Sanchez, the maid who had filled in for Mrs. Sykes. "He's phoning her now," Nan said.

The children watched as he dialed her number. Then he stood with the phone to his ear, listening. Finally he shook his head and hung up. "No answer."

"Gee, maybe we'll never find out what my mystery prize was," Freddie said wistfully.

Officer Tompkins rumpled the little

boy's curly blond hair. "We won't give up yet, sonny. Maybe the lady's just outside or someplace where she can't hear the phone. We'll drive over to her house and see. Or if she's gone shopping, she may be back when we get there. Come on, kids—won't take but a few minutes to find out!"

"Oh, goody!" said Flossie. "I'm glad there's still a chance to talk to her, aren't you, Freddie?"

"You bet! What's the good of winning a prize if you never get to know what it is?"

"That's right, young fella. And when we do find out, we'll stand a better chance of getting it back for you!"

But when they rang the bell at Miss Sanchez's house, nobody came to the door. A neighbor lady called over, "If you're looking for the Sanchezes, I think they're gone for the weekend."

Freddie sighed. "I guess I'm never going to see my prize," he said ruefully.

Bert gave his little brother a quick hug.

"Never mind, Freddie. We'll find out all about it sooner or later."

On the way back to the School Fair, Officer Tompkins decided to stop by the Lakeport Hospital. "We'll see if Bimbo the Clown feels well enough yet to ride back with us," he told the twins.

The Bobbseys, too, were eager to see how Bimbo was—especially since he had gotten hurt while trying to save Freddie's mystery prize. They followed the policeman into the hospital lobby, where he spoke to a lady at the reception counter. "How's Bimbo the Clown, ma'am? If the doctor says he's okay, we can drive him back to the fair."

"Oh, did you bring the clown here?" The reception clerk stared at the policeman in surprise.

Her odd manner brought an anxious look to his face. "Bimbo wasn't badly hurt, was he?" Officer Tompkins inquired hastily.

"I really don't know."

"Hasn't the doctor seen him yet?"

"No, Bimbo's not even here at the hospital." Seeing the policeman's puzzled expression, she went on, "Everyone noticed him when he first came in the door. After all, it's not every day you see a circus clown in full makeup! But he never stopped at the counter or said a word to anybody—just walked on past and down the hall."

The lady turned and gestured to a central corridor that looked as if it ran all the way through the building. "Afterward, I asked one of the hospital guards to check on him," she added. "He said the clown had just gone on out the back door. We couldn't figure it out!"

Neither could Officer Tompkins or the Bobbseys.

"Maybe Bimbo decided he just needed a walk in the fresh air to make him feel better," Nan suggested hopefully as they returned to the car.

The policeman shrugged. "Maybe so. I

suppose he could have strolled back through the park. We'll find out when we get to the school."

But it turned out that Bimbo had not returned to the fair. "Guess his clowning's over for today," said Bert. "His walk must not have helped much."

"Just think, we won't see him again for a whole year!" said Flossie, her little face solemn.

"I know." Nan gave her little sister's hand a squeeze. "Let's just hope he's all right."

Mr. and Mrs. Bobbsey had waited for the twins. But now they had to leave, Mrs. Bobbsey to do her weekend shopping and other household chores, while Mr. Bobbsey went off to his lumberyard, which was always busy on Saturdays.

The children, however, stayed on to enjoy Fun Day. Nan joined some of her girlfriends. Bert and his chum, Charlie Mason, went to try their luck at pitching horseshoes. Freddie and Flossie each had a ride on the pony and the Ferris wheel.

By now the little twins were feeling hungry, so they got hot dogs at the refreshment stand.

"Hey, here comes Rodney Blake," said Freddie.

The fat boy nodded hello to the little twins, then bought a hot dog and began to eat it.

"Who's tending Mister Checkers?" Freddie asked.

Rodney shrugged glumly. "Nobody. He beat everyone, so the kids got tired playing him."

The young computer whiz seemed lonesome and fidgety. Flossie had a hunch that Danny Rugg's bullying had spoiled Fun Day for him. She felt sorry for Rodney and said, "Freddie, do you think Mr. Gresham would mind if Rodney came and played in the tree house with us?"

"Golly, no—that's a great idea!" said

Freddie. "Have you ever been up in a tree house, Rodney?"

The plump boy shook his head and brightened up when the little twins invited him to join them.

The three set out from school, heading for Miss Wagby's mansion. Mr. Gresham had kept his promise, and a sturdy new ladder was now in place. Rodney climbed up first, then reached down and gave Freddie and Flossie each a hand as they clambered up on the tree house porch.

The house itself was surprisingly big and roomy. Besides shuttered windows and a door, it had children's furniture, and the floor was covered with carpeting. "Gee, this is wonderful," said Flossie, trying out a little rocking chair. "Somebody could almost *live* up here!"

"Looks like Miss Wagby's nephew *did* live up here sometimes," said Freddie.

There was a boy's sweater still lying in the tree house, as well as several toys and

some old books and magazines, and a worn, dirty pair of gym shoes that might have fitted Bert. Flossie also found a cute pink horse carved out of soap.

"He was a pretty good carver," said Rodney.

The three children played happily in the tree house for the rest of the afternoon. They were up high enough to see almost a block away, except where trees covered their view.

By the time they climbed down to walk home, Rodney Blake was quite cheerful and talkative. "It was really fun, playing up in that tree house! Thanks a lot for asking me," he told the Bobbseys.

"Who do you usually play with?" Freddie asked.

Rodney's smile faded. His shoulders slumped and he looked down at the pavement as they walked along. "Nobody," he mumbled.

"I don't think I've ever seen your folks," said Flossie, changing the subject.

"What kind of work does your daddy do?"

"He's an airline pilot."

Freddie's blue eyes widened with admiration. "Gee, that must be pretty exciting!"

Rodney shrugged. "I guess so ... except he's away from home so much, I don't see him very often. My mother's away a lot, too. She works for a company that makes perfume and stuff like that, and she goes around to different stores all over the country. In fact, I'll probably have to make my own supper tonight."

"Why don't you come and eat with us, then?" said Freddie.

Rodney Blake stopped and stared at the little blond boy. "Do you mean that?"

"Sure, why not?"

"How do you know your mom and dad would let me?"

The little twins grinned. "Don't worry," Flossie said with a giggle. "There's a lady named Dinah Johnson who helps my mother cook. They make lots of food—and it's real yummy! There'll be plenty to go around."

Mr. and Mrs. Bobbsey welcomed the little twins' new friend, and dinner was a happy time. Sometime later, the telephone rang and Dinah went to answer it. She came back looking somewhat surprised.

"A lady," she said, "wants to speak to Mr. Freddie Bobbsey!"

The Motel Clue

Wide-eyed, Freddie took the telephone receiver and said, "Hello, I'm Freddie Bobbsey."

"This is Rosa Sanchez. I worked for a while as Miss Wagby's maid," the caller told him. "I just read in the newspaper about the trouble at your School Fair. The story said your mystery prize was stolen."

"That's right." Freddie was hopefully excited. "Mrs. Sykes said you might know about the prize, so Officer

Tompkins took us to your house. But nobody was home."

"No, my family and I are staying at a cottage on the beach this weekend. That is why I called—to see if I could help in any way."

"What was the prize, Miss Sanchez?" Freddie could hardly wait to hear.

"A pink toy horse. Miss Wagby told me to wrap it and have Mr. Gresham take it to the school."

"Oh." Freddie felt a bit let down, especially after what he had heard about the kind old lady's mystery gifts. Somehow, a little toy horse did not seem like all that much of a prize.

"Anyhow, I will be back on Monday if Officer Tompkins wants to talk to me," the maid said.

"Okay. Thanks a lot for calling, Miss Sanchez," Freddie said politely and hung up. When he told the other Bobbseys, they, too, were somewhat surprised to learn what Miss Wagby had sent.

"Maybe it was a *windup* horse," said Flossie. "You'd like that, wouldn't you, Freddie?"

"Sure!" Freddie smiled more eagerly.

"But what if a seventh- or eighth-grader had won the prize? A toy horse wouldn't be much fun for an older kid," Bert pointed out.

"No, perhaps it might not have been very suitable in that case," said Mrs. Bobbsey. "Still, it's kind of Miss Wagby to donate any prize."

"Wait! I just had an idea," Nan mused aloud. "Remember how puzzled the housekeeper looked when we told her about the mystery prize being stolen?"

"What about it?" said Bert.

"Maybe that new maid made a mistake."

"How could she make a mistake?" asked Freddie. "She said Miss Wagby told her what to wrap."

"Even so," Nan persisted, "I think we should tell Mrs. Sykes."

After dinner, Rodney telephoned home to find out if his parents were back. His father had just arrived from the airport. Still wearing his pilot's uniform, Mr. Blake drove to the Bobbseys' house to pick up his bright young son. Before leaving, Roddie thanked the Bobbseys for inviting him to dinner.

"I really liked being here," he declared shyly.

Mrs. Bobbsey smiled. "We enjoyed having you, Rodney."

"Come back soon," Mr. Bobbsey added.

"Roddie just loved your corn fritters and banana cake, Dinah," Flossie said after the Blakes had left.

"Well, I'm glad," said the cook. "But I reckon he always gets plenty to eat. If you ask me, what that boy craves is more friends to play with and having his mamma and daddy home more often."

The long summer day was not yet over. Before twilight gathered, Nan set out for the Wagby mansion with the other three twins.

This time Mrs. Sykes answered the bell more quickly. "I was just watching television," she said. "Come in and tell me what I can do for you."

Nan related how Miss Sanchez had called and told Freddie the mystery prize was a pink toy horse. "That seemed different from the prizes she's sent before," Nan went on. "Then I remembered you saying she must have changed her mind, and I . . . well, I wondered if the maid might have wrapped the wrong thing by mistake."

"How do you mean, dear?"

"A pink toy horse sounds like one of those beautiful little statues and carvings Miss Wagby collects. Do you suppose—"

Before Nan could even finish, the housekeeper cried, "Oh, my stars!"

Looking horrified, Mrs. Sykes dashed into the parlor, just off the hall.

As she turned on the lights in the big, old high-ceilinged room, her mouth dropped open in dismay. "Oh, no!" she wailed. "It's gone! Miss Wagby's favorite pink jade carving!"

She sat down heavily in a chair, wringing her hands. "You were right, my dear," she said. "There certainly *was* a mistake. Miss Wagby would never give that pink jade horse away! I'd better phone the police!"

She rose and hurried to the telephone. The Bobbseys could hear her telling the policeman who answered that the stolen mystery prize was a very valuable jade carving.

Later, as the twins walked home, Bert said, "Boy, that was a good idea you had, Nan!"

"Yes," said Flossie. "Mrs. Sykes really 'preciulated' you telling her about the pink horse."

Bert chuckled. "You wouldn't by any chance mean she *appreciated* it, would you, kewpie doll?"

"Come on, Flossie! We'll just let those silly brothers of ours walk by themselves." Nan took her little sister's hand and they moved on ahead.

"Nan, do you 'spose Miss Wagby meant to send that pink horse in the tree house?" Flossie asked.

"The soap one you mentioned?" Nan smiled. "I doubt it. She probably doesn't even know it's up there."

On Sunday morning, the Bobbseys breakfasted on Dinah's pancakes, then left for church. After the sermon, the minister made a few announcements.

"Friends, as you know, I always visit any members of our flock who are ill in the hospital before our Sunday service. I'm happy to say Samantha Wagby is now on the mend. However, she was quite upset over some news she had just received. Perhaps you've heard how a mystery prize was stolen at the School Fair yesterday. It seems the prize package actually contained a valuable pink jade horse her maid had sent by mistake. So now Miss Wagby wants me to announce that she's offering a reward to anyone who can supply information that will help to get it back. A very substantial reward."

Later, there was a hum of conversation as the twins followed their parents up the aisle and out of the church. Flossie tugged Nan's arm.

"What does 'supstannal' mean?"

"A *big* reward, Flossie. And the word is 'substantial.' "

"Nan, that's what I said." The little girl gave her older sister a severe look.

That afternoon, Dinah needed some whipping cream for the chocolate cream pie she was baking as dessert for Sunday dinner. Bert biked to the supermarket to get some. There he saw Miss Wagby's handyman, Mr. Gresham, tacking up a reward notice for the jade horse on the store's bulletin board.

"We heard about that from the minister this morning," Bert remarked.

"Yep, Miss Wagby really prized that little pink horse," said the elderly handy-man. "She bought it on a trip to China. Worth a lot of money, I guess. She's even asked the police to send a reward notice to the *Lakeport News* and the TV and radio stations."

When Bert got home, he told the rest of the family about seeing Mr. Gresham. After dinner, the Bobbseys were sur-prised by hearing their doorbell ring.

Dinah answered it and ushered a middle-aged woman into the front room. "This lady, Mrs. Biller, wants to talk to you children," she said.

The visitor turned out to be a maid at the Cloverleaf Motel. She explained that she was out driving with her husband and had just heard the reward an-nouncement on their car radio. The

Bobbsey twins had been mentioned in the news broadcast, so she had looked up their address in the phone book.

"I wonder if any of you know what sort of box that jade horse was in?" Mrs. Biller asked.

"It was wrapped in red paper," Freddie piped up.

"Uh-oh! Then I think the thief stayed at the Cloverleaf Motel!" Mrs. Biller related that she had gone into room fifteen that morning to make the bed and change the towels. She had noticed a box containing some pink object. "It looked like a carved animal," she went on. "And there was some crumpled-up red wrapping paper beside it."

"Wow," Bert muttered. "That sure sounds like Freddie's mystery prize!"

Mrs. Biller nodded. "Yes, but just then the man in fifteen came back from breakfast. He got real mad when he saw me there. He covered up the box quick and told me to come back after he checked out."

"That could be very important information, Mrs. Biller," said Mr. Bobbsey. He had come into the living room in time to hear her story.

"My husband and I thought it might be," she said proudly.

Mrs. Bobbsey invited the Billers to have some coffee. But the visitor said she and her husband were on their way home to dinner, so she thought she had better go to the police station right away.

"Thanks for letting us know," the twins said.

Next morning at breakfast, all four Bobbsey children were in high spirits.

"Hooray!" said Freddie as he jumped up from the table after gobbling his cereal. "This is the last week of school!"

His big brother grinned. "Not even a whole week to go."

Bert was the first one out the door. But

he stopped short when he saw that a
piece of paper had been taped to it.
Words were lettered on the paper. They
read:

The crook who stole
the mystery prize was
really after ZYX!

·6·

Sidewalk Bully

Freddie and Flossie were wide-eyed when Bert read the sign to them aloud.

"What does 'ZYX' mean?" Freddie asked.

Bert shrugged. "Search me. Sounds like somebody's dumb idea of a joke."

Nan also was baffled. "I wonder who could have stuck that sign on our front door?" she said.

"Maybe Danny Rugg," Bert guessed.

On their way to school, the twins saw Officer Tompkins. They told him about the sign. He, too, thought it might be a prank by one of their schoolmates but promised to look into it.

"I guess you twins already know about that clue at the Cloverleaf Motel?" he went on.

"You mean that box the maid saw in room fifteen that looked like Freddie's prize?" asked Nan.

"Right. One of our detectives has checked out the facts. The man in room fifteen was tall and bald and signed his name as 'J. Smith' when he came to the motel."

"Gee, there must be a lot of people with that name!" said Bert.

"There sure are," Officer Tompkins agreed. "It may be phony, but they're trying to trace him."

The school year was nearly over, and Monday was exam day. Nan and Bert's grade took their math test in the computer room. Part of the test was to see how well they could use the machines.

Afterward, the principal brought a thin,

bony man into the room. His nose was crooked, which made Bert wonder if he might have been a boxer once. To Bert's surprise, the principal introduced him as Professor Tate of Midwest University.

"As some of you may know," the principal said proudly, "Professor Tate once taught general science at this very school. Later he studied and did research work for a number of years, and became a famous scientist himself. About two weeks ago, he donated this powerful computer to our school."

The principal gestured to a large machine on a stand in one corner of the room, and went on, "This computer can do much more than our present models. It will be useful to the teachers and me in running the school and planning classes. And I think you'll all be amazed at the things that can be drawn and displayed on its screen."

He asked Professor Tate to say a few words to the class. The professor's face seemed frozen in a rather severe expression. He looked as if he had worked hard all his life and had not had much fun or much time to enjoy himself.

He explained that Midwest University had ordered a special new computer to aid him in his lab work, so he had decided to donate this one to the school where he had once taught.

"I'm now on summer vacation," Professor Tate went on, "but I happened to be passing through Lakeport, so I stopped in to see if the computer had been delivered safely. I will present it to the school officially on Wednesday when the graduating class get their diplomas."

When he finished speaking, the students all clapped. Professor Tate tried to smile, but his face still looked rather frozen and severe.

"I'll bet he was a tough teacher and a hard marker," Bert murmured to his sister after the class filed out.

Nan was not so sure. "Personally I

thought he seemed rather nice," she mused. "If we'd been his pupils, I have a hunch we might have liked him."

Bert shrugged. "Well, he sure *looked* like a tough teacher."

"Maybe he's just shy," Nan said sympathetically.

During recess, Freddie and Flossie looked for Rodney Blake. But a boy in his class told them Rodney had not come to school that day.

"Maybe he's sick," Flossie said, with a worried look on her rosy-cheeked little face.

"Let's go to his house and find out after school," said Freddie.

"Okay, that's a good idea."

To their surprise, no one answered when they rang the Blakes' doorbell that afternoon.

On their way home, Freddie muttered, "Uh-oh! Look who's coming."

Danny Rugg was walking toward them with a friend. From the look on the bully's face, it was plain to Freddie and Flossie that he had not forgotten the way Bert had stopped him from punching Rodney Blake. Both could see that he intended to take out his grudge on them.

"Where do you think *you're* going?" Danny said, planting himself in the little twins' path.

"Home," said Freddie, trying not to sound as scared as he felt.

"That's what *you* think, half-pint." Danny grinned unpleasantly, and his friend snickered.

"Let us go by, you bad boy!" Flossie scolded.

As she and Freddie tried to walk around their two tormentors, Danny and his friend reached out to grab the small twins.

"Hold it, you two," said a voice behind them. "You lay a hand on those kids, and you'll both get punched in the jaw!"

The two big boys stopped as suddenly as if they had gotten their hands too close

to a hot radiator. Turning, they saw Bert Bobbsey hurrying toward them. His pal, Charlie Mason, was with him, and both had their fists clenched.

"Aw, pipe down," Danny blustered. "Nobody's touching the little brats!"

"Lucky for you you didn't," Bert said grimly. "Now beat it!"

Danny and his friend glared at the other two boys, but did not dare to risk a fight. After a moment they walked off with sullen sneers.

Freddie gulped to Bert and Charlie, "Boy, am I ever glad you guys came along!"

Bert chuckled and tousled his little brother's blond hair. "Don't worry. Those creeps won't bother you for a while. They know what they'll get if they do!"

Flossie asked where he and Charlie were going.

"We were looking for you two," said Bert. "Dinah wants to know if you'd like to go for a drive in the country with her and Sam."

"You bet!" Freddie said, and Flossie chimed in eagerly, "Where are they going?"

Dinah's husband, Sam Johnson, worked at Mr. Bobbsey's lumberyard, but Bert said that he was taking the afternoon off so Dinah could shop for fresh fruits and vegetables at farmers' roadside stands. "Dinah wants to make something special for dinner tomorrow to celebrate the end of school," he explained.

"Oh, goodie!" cried Flossie. But her face fell when Bert added that Mr. and Mrs. Bobbsey would not be at home to enjoy the dinner.

"Dad's going to a lumbermen's convention in Cleveland, and Mom's going with him."

This was less welcome news, but the little twins rushed home eagerly to go with the Johnsons.

That evening all four twins were

watching TV. They saw a commercial for a circus that had just come to Cleveland, which made them think of clowns.

"I wonder why Bimbo went away without telling anyone?" said Flossie.

"He probably wasn't feeling very well after that fall downstairs," Bert replied.

"Then why didn't he want to see the doctor?"

"Another thing," said Freddie, "how did he know that crook would try to steal my prize?"

"You mean, how did he know beforehand?"

"Sure." Freddie nodded. "He must have, 'cause that lady, Mrs. Cole, said he was holding the box, and the crook was trying to grab it."

"Hmm," mused Bert. "Now that you mention it, that's a good question. If we knew where Bimbo went, maybe he could help solve the whole mystery."

Nan snapped her fingers. "Golly, that gives me a dynamite idea!"

"Let's hear it," said her twin.

"What's the best place to look for a clown?"

"At a circus!" Flossie giggled.

"Right!" said Nan. "So why don't we ask Mom and Dad if they'll take us to Cleveland with them tomorrow, and let us go to the circus?"

Her idea brought cheers from her brothers and sister. When they asked their parents, Mr. and Mrs. Bobbsey looked at each other.

"Why not, Dick?" Mary Bobbsey said to her husband. "They only have a half day of school, so they could leave with us right after lunch."

Mr. Bobbsey smiled. "As you say, why not?"

More cheers followed from all four twins.

"Oh, boy!" said Freddie as he and Flossie climbed the stairs at bedtime. "I can hardly wait till tomorrow!"

Startling News

"I don't see why we have to go to school today at all," Freddie blurted at the breakfast table the next morning.

"Oh, Freddie, this last day is always fun, isn't it, Bert?" said Nan, picking up a crispy piece of bacon with her fork.

"It sure is! Just half a day, Freddie, and sometimes the teacher brings a treat for the class, or you play games."

"I know why Freddie doesn't want to go to school," Flossie cut in. "He can't wait to get to the circus, and neither can I!"

"If you children don't eat your breakfast, you won't have strength to go anywhere," Dinah scolded. "Remember, you'll only have time for a quick lunch at noon. So eat up!"

Later that morning, Freddie and Flossie found out that Nan and Bert were right. School *was* fun! Right in the middle of a guessing game, the wall phone rang. Their teacher answered it. When she hung up, she said that the principal wished to see Freddie and Flossie Bobbsey in his office.

"I wonder why he wants to see us?" Freddie muttered on their way through the hall.

"Oh, Freddie, don't worry. We'll soon find out," Flossie said as she opened the office door.

Inside, Mrs. Bunting, the clerk, smiled and asked them to take a seat on the long wooden bench opposite the attendance counter.

On a chair nearby sat a tallish man with

a bald head and glasses. He wore a business suit and had a briefcase. He smiled and winked at the twins and joked, "Never mind if you've been naughty, kids. They probably won't punish you much on the last day of school."

Flossie and Freddie smiled back at him politely. He was very talkative and introduced himself as Mr. Defister. He said he had some new computers to sell that would make learning fun, so boys and girls like Freddie and Flossie would enjoy coming to school.

"Oh, we like school," said Flossie. At this, Mr. Defister laughed and winked. Flossie thought he winked an awful lot. At first she supposed it was just his way of being jolly, but it made her feel uncomfortable. Later, she decided it might be a habit that he hardly even realized he had.

Presently they heard a buzz, and Mrs. Bunting said, "You Bobbsey twins can go in the office now."

"Good luck, kids!" Mr. Defister smiled and winked as they got up from the bench.

In the principal's office, a well-dressed man and woman were seated facing his desk. "Mr. and Mrs. Blake here have a problem," the principal said after greeting the small twins. "We're hoping you can help them."

On hearing the couple's name, Freddie and Flossie suddenly realized that Mr. Blake was Rodney's father. They had not recognized him because he was wearing an ordinary suit instead of an airline pilot's uniform.

"Their son Rodney is missing," the principal went on.

"Ooh!" gasped Flossie.

"We know you're friends of Rodney's," said Mr. Blake. "That's why we thought he might have told you something . . . something that would give us a clue to where he's gone."

Mrs. Blake added, "The last time we

saw him was on Sunday, when we were all home together. His daddy and I both work, and unfortunately our schedules overlap. So we didn't realize until this morning that neither of us had seen Rodney yesterday."

She paused tearfully to wipe her eyes with a handkerchief, and Mr. Blake took up the story. "In other words, we don't know how long Rodney's been gone. What makes us worry even more is this note we found in his room."

Mr. Blake showed the twins a piece of paper. Printed on it in big letters were the words:

BETTER KEEP
YOUR TRAP
SHUT, KID,
ABOUT WHAT
YOU SAW AT
SCHOOL OR
IT'S THE LAST
TIME YOU'LL
EVER OPEN IT!

The twins' eyes widened anxiously as Mr. Blake read the unpleasant message aloud.

"Golly, that sounds awful!" wailed Flossie.

Mrs. Blake nodded and could not keep a sob from her voice. "You can imagine how frightened we are for his safety."

"The last time we saw Rodney was on Saturday night when he had dinner at our house," said Freddie.

"Yesterday we went to your place to find out why Rodney didn't come to school," Flossie related, "but no one answered the door."

Mr. Blake looked worriedly at his wife. "I guess we'd better go to the police."

"Yes, I would certainly advise that," said the principal.

Mr. and Mrs. Blake thanked the twins and promised to let them know as soon as they had word about their missing son.

"Do you suppose Rodney's been *kidnapped*?" Flossie murmured in a hushed

voice as she and Freddie walked back
down the hall to their schoolroom.

Her little brother shook his head
helplessly. "Search me. But I sure hope
he's all right!"

"So do I!" said Flossie.

Soon afterward, the air rang with happy
shouts and laughter as school let out for
summer vacation.

After a hurried lunch, the Bobbsey
twins and their mother and father got into
the car for the drive to Cleveland. Freddie and Flossie were so excited they almost forgot to tell the rest of the family
about Rodney Blake's disappearance.

"Oh, my, his poor parents!" Mrs.
Bobbsey sighed after hearing the story.

"We'll all help look for him when we
get back," Nan promised, and Bert
agreed.

When they arrived in Cleveland, Mr.
Bobbsey pulled up in front of the circus
grounds. It was still half an hour before
the show was scheduled to begin under

the big top, but he had arranged through a business friend in the city for the twins to be admitted early.

He got out of the car and took his four children up to the gate, where he spoke to the man at the ticket booth and paid for their tickets. Then he said to the twins, "Now stay together! Your mother will pick you up after the performance and bring you to the hotel where the convention's being held. Okay?"

The twins nodded eagerly. Then, after waving good-bye to their father, they went on in through the gate. A brass band was playing, and a noisy crowd was already milling about the midway.

"First let's try to find out about Bimbo," Bert suggested. He spoke to a passing roustabout—or circus worker—who directed them to the trailer van the clowns used as a dressing room.

An elderly clown in full makeup had just come out of the trailer. "Excuse me," Bert said to him, "but do you know a clown named Bimbo?"

Nan had spent part of the morning in school drawing a picture of Bimbo with colored crayons. Flossie and Freddie thought it looked just like him. But when she showed it to the clown, he stared at it for a few moments, then pursed his lips and shook his head regretfully.

"Nope," he said. "Most circus clowns are friends. We know each other's acts and costumes. But I've never seen a clown like him, or known one named Bimbo."

The twins thanked him and turned away, disappointed. But Nan slowed her steps and finally stopped before they had gone very far. She frowned and said in a low voice, "I'm not sure I believe that clown."

"How come?" said Bert.

"I'm not sure. Just the way he took a while before he answered, I guess. Somehow I have a feeling he was covering up."

"Why should he do that?" Bert argued. "Bimbo hasn't done anything wrong."

"He even got hurt trying to save my mystery prize from that thief!" Freddie chimed in.

"I know, but it won't hurt to double-check." Nan stopped a circus dancer in pink tights and a spangled costume as she was hurrying by and showed her the crayon sketch of Bimbo. "Do you know this clown?" she asked.

The dancer needed only a quick glance at the drawing before she smiled and replied, "Of course! He belongs to our circus. That's good old Honker!"

·8·

The Red-Nosed Clown

The dancer hurried on as the twins looked at one another excitedly. "Nan, you were right!" said Flossie. "How did you ever guess?"

"Just lucky." Nan smiled back at her little sister. "Come on, everyone! Let's get to our seats and watch the show. We can see if Honker is in the performance."

The big tent was already filling up, but the twins found good seats next to an aisle. Soon the brass band broke into a rousing march, and the circus performers began parading into the show rings—

dancers and bareback riders, horses and elephants, acrobats and clowns.

But Bimbo, or Honker, was not among them!

Bert leaned over and whispered to Nan, "Watch my seat for a while, okay?"

"Where are you going, Bert?"

"Back to the clowns' trailer to look for Bimbo. I have a hunch that first clown warned him we were looking for him, and that's why he's staying out of sight. But now that the show's started, maybe he won't be so careful."

"I want to come with you!" said Freddie.

"Well ... all right," Bert said. "But stick close to me all the time."

The two boys left the stand and walked toward the entrance of the tent. The attendant on duty assured them they could get back in with no trouble as long as they held on to their ticket stubs. Soon they were hurrying across the midway toward the circus wagons and trailers.

There was no one in sight around the clowns' trailer. The boys managed to sneak closer without being seen. Peering in through a window, they saw a long counter with makeup mirrors, stools, bunks, and chairs strewn with clothing. There were also several trunks belonging to the various clowns. One trunk bore the name Honker!

Bert could see no one inside, so he hissed to Freddie, "Come on! Maybe we can find some clue that will tell us who Bimbo or Honker *really* is!"

He pushed the door open cautiously and they slipped into the trailer. They were just about to delve into Honker's trunk when they heard footsteps on the gritty ground outside. Bert grabbed Freddie's arm and shushed him to silence.

The steps came closer, up to the trailer door.

"Get down, Freddie!" Bert whispered and pushed his little brother to the floor.

Both boys peeked around the trunk at the person who entered.

It was Bimbo the Clown!

For a moment Bert wasn't sure what to do next. Then he decided to stand up and let himself be seen. He pulled Freddie to his feet, also. After all, Bimbo was the person they had come to see.

The clown stared at them in surprise. He took off his squashed top hat and scratched his wig. Then he rested one elbow on his other hand and scowled, as if trying to figure out what the boys were doing there. After a while he lifted his tattered coat and started scratching himself on the side.

Freddie began to giggle. The clown smiled happily. He tapped the alarm clock that was strapped around his wrist and pointed off toward the big top as if urging the boys to hurry.

"I guess you're wondering why we aren't watching the show," said Bert. "Well, *we're* wondering why *you* aren't performing today. Is it because that other clown warned you someone was looking for you?"

Bimbo stared down at his big floppy shoes. Then he shrugged and began to caper about. He tossed his hat in the air, caught it on the tip of his cane, and began to twirl it.

Bert could see that the clown did not intend to reply. But Nan was so kind-hearted and sympathetic, people always seemed willing to talk to *her*. Maybe she could coax Bimbo to speak.

"Look, Mr. Bimbo or Honker, whatever your name is," Bert said aloud. "Would you please stay here while I go get my sisters? They'd like to see you, too." To his little brother, he added, "You stay here, Freddie."

Bert dashed out of the trailer. Bimbo did not try to stop him. While he was gone, the clown juggled makeup jars and brushes and all sorts of things while Freddie laughed and clapped.

Presently Bert returned with Nan and Flossie. "Bimbo!" the girls exclaimed. The clown stopped juggling and bowed low to greet them.

Then suddenly he recognized Flossie as the little kewpie-doll girl at the School Fair. "Ah, my beautiful princess!" he cried.

Next moment he clasped her hand, circled her waist, and began waltzing her gaily around the trailer. Her blond curls fluttered about her head!

Then he picked up the squealing, giggling little girl and bounced her high in the air, catching her as she came down!

Flossie shook with laughter. "Now honk your nose for us, please, Bimbo!" she begged.

The clown punched his squashed top hat into shape, clasped it on his head, scratched his back with his cane, did a few dance steps with his cane swinging on one arm, and suddenly squeezed his nose. A loud *honk!* was heard, which sent all the Bobbseys into laughter.

But Bert noticed that Bimbo had stuck his other hand into one of his roomy coat pockets. I'll bet he's got an old-fashioned car horn in there! thought Bert.

Freddie was hopping up and down excitedly. "May I try honking your nose?" he shouted. And without waiting for permission, he jumped up and grabbed Bimbo's big red nose.

But instead of honking, it turned out to be a red rubber ball just stuck on with putty. It came off in Freddie's hand!

Now the Bobbseys could see Bimbo's real nose. It was crooked—just like another nose the older twins had seen that very morning.

Nan gasped, *"Professor Tate!"*

9

Secret Hobby

The professor sighed and sat down. "Yes, my dear," he said with a sad, funny clown smile, "you've discovered my secret."

Freddie was still bewildered at the way Bimbo's nose had turned into a rubber ball. "I d-don't understand," he gasped. "Does Nan mean you're really that professor who's giving our school a big computer?"

"Yes, my boy—and she's quite right."

"But I don't understand, either," said Bert. "I mean, if you're a professor . . .

well . . . how come you're a clown, too?"

"I know, I know." Professor Tate nodded ruefully. "It must seem very odd. But you see, I was never a very good teacher, I'm afraid. My students always considered me cold and grumpy—and maybe I was. I wanted to be warm and jolly, so they would like me . . . but I didn't know how."

"*I* like you," said Flossie. "And I think you're the funniest clown I ever saw!"

"Thank you, dear. I'm glad if you do!" Professor Tate alias Bimbo gave his kewpie-doll princess a quick hug. "I suppose that's why I secretly wanted to be a clown . . . so that someday pupils might feel that way about me."

He said he had been afraid that practicing to be a clown would make him seem ridiculous, especially after he became a college professor. So he could only pursue his hobby during summer vacations.

"I studied clowning at a circus school in Florida," Professor Tate went on.

"And of course I always enjoyed doing my clown act at the Lakeport School Fair, where nobody knew who I was. That way I could be as silly and undignified as I liked. And finally I was allowed to join this circus troupe on their summer tours."

"But they call you by a different name," said Nan.

"That's right, my dear." The professor smiled. "Honker is my professional name. But I'm always Bimbo at your school's Fun Day."

Bert had been looking around the trailer while Professor Tate was speaking. His glance fell on a thick brown envelope in the clown's open trunk. It bore the label ZYX printed in big letters.

Bert gasped as he suddenly remembered the sign taped to the Bobbseys' front door: *The crook who stole the mystery prize was really after ZYX!*

"Excuse me, Professor," he blurted, pointing to the envelope in the trunk, "but does that name have anything to do with your fight with the thief at the School Fair?"

"It does indeed." The professor nodded.

"Would you mind telling us about it, please?" Nan requested.

"Well now, it's a long story. You see, I've been working on an important chemical formula. It will help to make a strong new material that can take the place of steel. But I knew all along that many companies would like to get hold of such a formula. So I code-named my laboratory work 'Project ZYX' to keep it a secret from any industrial spies."

Freddie's blue eyes grew big and round. "Did any spies try to steal your secret?"

"Yes sirree, one did," declared Professor Tate. "He broke into my lab once and I almost caught him, but he got away. I got a good look at him, though, and nicknamed him Blinky."

"Did he ever try again?" Flossie asked.

"He certainly did, honey. He even broke into this circus trailer, but I fooled him."

The professor said that a company now wanted to buy his formula, but the terms would take several months to arrange. Meantime, he feared Blinky would try to rob his lab again during summer vacation, while the deal was being worked out.

"So I put the formula on a floppy disk," he explained, "and stored it in that computer I gave your school. Then I destroyed all other copies of the formula. But to fool Blinky I put that envelope in my circus trunk and labeled it ZYX."

"If he broke into the trailer," said Bert, "how come the envelope is still here?"

Professor Tate chuckled. "Because the envelope was stuffed with computer printout paper that had nothing to do with my formula. A few days ago I came back here to change after a performance, and the printout paper was gone. Instead, the envelope was stuffed with newspaper pages."

Nan's eyes twinkled. "You mean Blinky stole the wrong stuff?"

"Exactly. You can imagine how mad he must have been when he found out all the data on that printout paper meant absolutely nothing!"

"Then he's still on your trail?" asked Bert.

"Definitely! On Fun Day I spotted him sneaking into the school. I was sure he'd guessed the hiding place of my formula. So I rushed into the school and grabbed that red paper-wrapped box from the storeroom. I was trying to fool Blinky and make him think the floppy disk was in the box."

"And your trick worked, didn't it, Bimbo?" Freddie enthused, his eyes still big.

"Yes, Blinky ran up and snatched the box from me and pushed me downstairs," the clown-professor said. "I'm sorry about your prize, though, Freddie."

"Me, too," said the little Bobbsey boy.

"Well, never mind. We'll try to get everything sorted out." Professor Tate smiled. He seemed much more cheerful now that he had told his story. He took the twins back to the big top for the show and promised to treat them to dinner afterward.

The four Bobbseys enjoyed every minute of the circus. The thrilling highwire stunts and the lion tamer's act had them breathless. And the clowns and riders and performing animals left them happy and laughing.

After the show, while they waited for Professor Tate, Flossie and Freddie whispered together. Nan and Bert were too busy watching the roustabouts down on the circus floor to pay much attention, but when Professor Tate arrived, the blond, curly-haired twins were fairly bursting with excitement.

"Flossie and I have figured out something," Freddie told him importantly.

"But first we have to ask you a question," said Flossie. "Why'd you nickname Blinky Blinky?"

"Because he blinks his eyes a lot," said the professor.

Bert was somewhat puzzled at the little twins' remarks. "Well, we know that guy at the Cloverleaf Motel was tall and bald—" he began.

"So was that Mr. Defister we saw in the principal's office," Flossie interrupted. "We thought he kept winking at us. But now I'll bet he couldn't help it—he was *blinking!*"

"Whoa! Wait a minute," said Professor Tate. "Who's this Mr. Defister?"

"Well, he told us he wanted to sell the school some new computers," Freddie said.

The older twins looked at each other and snapped their fingers at the same time.

"Wow! That was probably just an excuse to help him find out where the computer room at school is located," exclaimed Bert.

"And most of all where to find that computer you donated, Professor Tate!" said Nan.

As the professor stared in dismay at the Bobbseys, Bert went on, "This probably means he's planning to come back and steal your floppy disk from the computer after the school is closed!"

10

Computer Room Mystery

"We'd better phone the Lakeport Police Department right away," said Nan, "and tell them to be on the lookout for that crook!"

"Right," Bert agreed. "I saw a phone booth just outside the gate when we first drove up. We can call from there."

Many of the people who had come to the circus were still roving about the midway; others were leaving, now that the afternoon performance was over. The Bobbseys and Professor Tate joined the laughing, chattering throng that was slowly streaming out through the gate.

While Bert was telephoning the police, Flossie cried, "Oh, goody! Here comes Mom!"

Mrs. Bobbsey had just parked across from the circus grounds and was getting out of the family car to collect her children. As the twins waved, she waved back and hurried to join them.

She was startled when Nan and the little twins introduced her to Professor Tate and told her all that had happened. As they finished their story, Bert came out of the phone booth.

"The police want Professor Tate and Freddie and Flossie to come back to Lakeport to help identify Blinky if he's caught," Bert reported.

"But I can't drive you all the way home right now," Mrs. Bobbsey said unhappily. "Daddy's expecting us at the hotel."

"No problem," Professor Tate assured her. "I have a car, and I've already promised to treat the twins to dinner. Would it be all right if *I* drove them back to Lakeport?"

Mrs. Bobbsey readily agreed. After kissing and hugging her four children and waving good-bye, she drove off to rejoin her husband.

It was a few minutes past seven o'clock when Professor Tate and the twins arrived back in Lakeport. They drove straight to police headquarters.

"No sign of our man yet," the police chief informed them, "but all officers and patrol cars have been alerted to watch out for him."

"What about Rodney Blake?" asked Freddie.

"We heard in school today that he is missing," Flossie explained. "Has he been found yet?"

"No, honey, I'm sorry to say he hasn't," the police chief replied. "But the whole force is keeping a lookout for him, too."

"Well, children," Professor Tate said, "since there's no one for us to identify yet, what about dinner? As I recall, there's a restaurant on West Street that serves delicious Chinese food . . . if that appeals to you?"

"No, wait, please," said Nan. "As long as we're here in Lakeport, why not come with us and be our guest for dinner?"

"Oh, yes, please come!" Flossie begged, clapping her hands. "We have a lady named Mrs. Johnson who lives with us and cooks the yummiest food!"

"Well . . ." Professor Tate smiled with pleasure at the invitation, but hesitated. "She won't be expecting us."

"She will if I call her first," said Nan, and then politely asked if she could use the phone at the police station.

Dinah chuckled when she heard Nan's request. "You don't even have to ask, dear. Your mother's already called and advised me to expect company!"

Professor Tate ate heartily, enjoying every mouthful of Dinah's fried chicken and biscuits and peach pie. "You were right, Flossie," he declared, sitting back and patting his vest. "That's the yummiest dinner I've eaten in years!"

The children all laughed, and Dinah beamed with satisfaction at his praise.

Nan, however, had been thoughtful throughout the meal. "When you scuffled with Blinky," she asked the professor, "was that code name ZYX mentioned by any chance?"

Professor Tate nodded. "Yes, I mentioned it on purpose as part of my trick to fool the thief. When he saw me clutching that red paper-wrapped box, I shouted, 'You won't get ZYX if I can help it!' How did you guess, my dear?"

"Because I have a hunch that may explain another part of the mystery." Nan told him about Rodney Blake being a computer whiz, and went on, "He may have examined that computer you're giving the school, and discovered the floppy disk with your formula stored on it. If he did—and if he saw you fighting Blinky and heard what you said—then he may have figured out what the thief was really after!"

"Hey, you're right, Nan!" Bert exclaimed with a look of excitement. "So Rodney could be the one who taped that sign on our door!"

"Yes, and that's not all," said Nan. "If Blinky saw Rodney watching, maybe he sent him that threatening note Freddie and Flossie told us about!"

Just then the phone rang. Bert answered it and came back looking more excited than ever. "That was the police," he said. "Someone just phoned in and reported seeing that spooky light at the school again!"

The twins and their guest sped to the school in the professor's car. A police car had pulled up just a moment before, and the light was still glowing on the upper floor of the school.

"That's the computer room!" cried Bert. But at that very moment, the light went out!

"Never mind, we have a key," said one police officer with a sergeant's stripes on his sleeves. "We'll soon find out who's up there!"

The two policemen and Professor Tate and the older twins all rushed inside. They switched on the lights and dashed upstairs. But the computer room was empty! Nor could they find any sign of the mysterious intruder.

Freddie and Flossie had stayed outside on Bert and Nan's orders. But the two little twins were quivering with excitement when the group finally rejoined them.

"W-w-we saw someone run out of the school!" Freddie blurted.

Flossie chimed in, her eyes as big as saucers, "And he was chasing a *ghost*!"

11

Surprise Prize

"Now hold on," said the police sergeant. "Let's get this straight. You saw two people come running out of the school?"

"Just *one* was a people," Flossie insisted. "The other was a *ghost!*"

And Freddie nodded emphatically. "He was smaller, and he was *all white!*"

Nan snapped her fingers. "I'll bet that was Rodney Blake!"

"You mean that missing boy?" the sergeant inquired. "The one who got the threatening note?"

"Right," said Bert. "He's crazy about computers. Rodney could be the one who sneaked into the school that other night when we saw a light in the computer room. He probably brought a sheet or a flour bag or something like that, to keep from being recognized if anyone spotted him!"

The two policemen exchanged quick glances.

"If the Bobbseys are right," said the police-car driver, "he must have escaped from his kidnapper!"

"The guy chasing him may *be* his kidnapper," the sergeant replied. "The boy's probably running home. Come on, let's drive to the Blakes' house and find out!"

"Well, well, well," murmured Professor Tate. "What an exciting evening this has turned out to be!"

"But those policemen are wrong," Freddie declared after a hasty, whispered conference with his twin. "We know where Rodney *really* went, don't we, Flossie?"

His little blond sister nodded eagerly. "We're pretty sure we do, anyhow. We don't think he was *ever* kidnapped."

"What do you mean?" Bert asked, staring at the small twins.

Freddie turned to Professor Tate. "Please drive us to Miss Wagby's house, and we'll show you what we mean!"

"Very well, my boy, but you'll have to show me where she lives."

"Uh-oh!" Nan murmured as they started off a moment later in the professor's car. "I'll bet I know what Freddie and Flossie mean!"

By the time they pulled up in the driveway of Samantha Wagby's mansion, Bert also had guessed what his little brother and sister were thinking.

The small twins were the first to jump out of the car. As they ran toward the grove of trees on one side of the mansion, Flossie explained, "If we're right, Rod-

ney's been hiding in the *tree house!*"

Very soon everyone knew that she and Freddie were, indeed, right. A man had climbed up the ladder to the tree house, and Rodney could be seen in the bright moonlight, clinging to a slender branch high above him!

The man was balancing on tiptoe on the tree house railing as he reached up and tried to shake Rodney loose. "Come on down, you brat, and give me that floppy disk," he snarled, "unless you'd rather take a good hard fall!"

The crook's snarl ended in a startled gasp as he saw Professor Tate and the Bobbseys come running up to the tree.

"Leave that boy alone, you scoundrel," the professor shouted angrily, "or you'll end up behind bars—provided I don't get hold of you first!"

Nan and Flossie ran to the mansion to get help or phone the police. Mr. Gresham the handyman, who lived in the servants' quarters, came to the door. On

hearing the girls' story, he ran out to help
the professor and the boys.

But very little help was needed. The
crook, blinking nervously, had tried to
jump down from the tree house and get
away. He had landed hard and fallen on
one knee. Before he could spring up and
run off, however, Professor Tate and Bert
and even little Freddie piled on top of
him, pinning him down!

Seeing Mr. Gresham arrive to join in
the struggle, Blinky gave up with a groan
of despair and allowed himself to be tied.

By this time Rodney Blake had managed to climb down safely from the tree
branch. While the group waited for the
police to arrive, Rodney told his rescuers
the whole story.

As Nan and Bert had guessed, he had
been so fascinated by the big computer
that he had sneaked back into the school
after dark to play with it, both tonight and
on the Friday evening before Fun Day.

"How did you get in?" Freddie asked him.

"I unlocked the window down in the boiler room during school. The janitor never noticed it."

The twins had been right on all counts. Rodney said he had discovered the floppy disk in the computer on Friday evening. Then, on Fun Day, when no one wanted to play Mister Checkers, he had gone into the school to get a drink at the fountain and had seen Bimbo fighting Blinky. When he heard what Bimbo shouted, he had guessed what the thief was after, because the floppy disk was labeled ZYX.

Rodney also knew the thief had caught a glimpse of him watching. Unluckily, Blinky had recognized him as the boy who had programmed the computer game. So on Sunday night, after getting the scary warning note, Rodney had stuck the sign on the Bobbseys' front door and gone off to hide in the tree house.

Normally, only eighth-graders were on hand for graduation day. But on Wednesday morning, the four Bobbsey twins were all in the school auditorium at the special invitation of the principal.

Just before the diplomas were handed out, Professor Tate officially presented the big computer to the Lakeport School. The audience clapped loudly—and clapped even louder when the principal revealed that the famed scientist was also the school's beloved clown, Bimbo!

Rodney Blake blushed proudly when he, too, got a hearty round of applause for foiling the crook's attempt to steal Professor Tate's valuable formula.

Then Freddie Bobbsey was called up on the stage. "And now, my boy"—the principal beamed—"here is the mystery prize for which you've waited so long!"

He handed Freddie a pink horse cut out of cardboard. On the back of it was a message in Samantha Wagby's delicate handwriting, which the principal read out to the whole audience:

> "Your prize is a
> course of riding
> lessons at the
> Lakeport Riding
> Academy!"

The principal told how Miss Wagby's temporary maid had mistaken her instructions and sent the jade horse by mistake. "And by the way," he added, "that jade horse was found in the thief's car . . . after the criminal had been caught and arrested, thanks to clever detective work by the Bobbsey twins!"

He then called the other three twins up on stage to stand beside Freddie as the audience clapped and cheered. For a moment the children felt sad that the mystery had been solved so quickly. But another one, just as challenging, would come along soon that would involve them all in *The Scarecrow Mystery.*

Freddie whispered to Flossie, "I wish we could get out of here!"

"Why?" she whispered back. "Don't you like people to know we're good detectives?"

Freddie fidgeted impatiently. "Sure—but I want to go horsie-back riding!"